P. Crumble and Jonathan Bentley

WE ARE ALL EQUAL

SCHOLASTIC

We are all EQUAL

Your day's not like mine

I chew on bamboo

You swing on a vine.

We are all EQUAL

You've crossed land and sea

Now this is your home

We share this country.

We are all EQUAL

With kids we adore

Though we are parents

Our lives aren't worth more.

We are all EQUAL

Your house may be small

I am not better

With room to stand tall.

We are all EQUAL

You can't walk or run

It doesn't take legs

To have lots of fun.

We are all EQUAL

You're shaped unlike me

I'm small and slender

You're strong and sturdy.

We are all EQUAL

Our love we decide

We can get married

No love is denied.

We are all EQUAL
You're kind and carefree
Beauty is deeper
Than what you can see.

We are all EQUAL

But you're not as strong

Bullying is not

The way to belong.

We are all EQUAL

If only you knew

Tests cannot measure

The good you will do.

We are all EQUAL
Let's shout it out loud

We share hopes and dreams
We're equal and proud.

To all those who take steps each day to create a more equal world – PC

For Clive and Neil – JB

Published in the UK by Scholastic Children's Books 2020
Euston House, 24 Eversholt Street, London, NW1 1DB
A division of Scholastic Limited

London – New York – Toronto – Sydney - Auckland
Mexico City – New Delhi – Hong Kong

SCHOLASTIC and associated logos are trademarks and/or
registered trademarks of Scholastic Inc.

First published in 2018 by Omnibus Books, an imprint of Scholastic Australia Pty Limited

Text © P. Crumble, 2018
Illustrations © Jonathan Bentley, 2018

The right of P. Crumble and Jonathan Bentley to be identified
as the author and illustrator of this work has been asserted by them under the Copyright,
Designs and Patents Act 1988.

ISBN 978 0702 30244 2

A CIP catalogue record for this book is available from the British Library.

Printed in China

Papers used by Scholastic Children's Books are made from wood grown in sustainable
forests.

10 9 8 7 6 5 4 3 2 1

www.scholastic.co.uk